ZOO DOINGS

Animal Poems by
JACK PRELUTSKY

Illustrated by
Paul O. Zelinsky

ZOO DOINGS

Greenwillow Books, New York

Library of Congress Cataloging in Publication Data
Prelutsky, Jack.   Zoo doings.
Summary: A collection of forty-six animal poems.
1. Animals—Juvenile poetry.   2. Children's poetry,
American.   [1. Animals—Poetry. 2. American poetry]
I. Zelinsky, Paul O., ill.   II. Title.
PS3566.R36A6 1983   811'.54   82-11996
ISBN 0-688-01782-7   ISBN 0-688-01784-3 (lib. bdg.)

To the Bronx Zoo

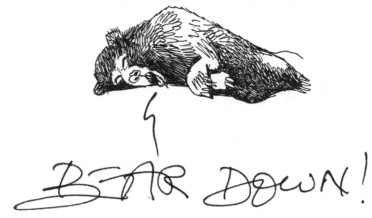

BEAR DOWN!

192

CONTENTS

ZOO DOINGS

LONG
GONE

Don't waste your time in looking for
the long-extinct tyrannosaur,
because this ancient dinosaur
just can't be found here anymore.

This also goes for stegosaurus,
allosaurus, brontosaurus
and any other saur or saurus.
They all lived here long before us.

A GOPHER
IN THE
GARDEN

There's a gopher in the garden, and he's
eating all the onions,
and he's eating all the broccoli and all the
beets and beans,
and he's eating all the carrots, all the corn and
cauliflower,
all the parsley, peas and pumpkins, all the
radishes and greens.

At breakfast, lunch or dinnertime the gopher is
    no loafer
and he quickly will devour everything
    before his eyes.
He does not even hesitate to eat a cabbage twice
    his weight,
or a watermelon five or six or seven
    times his size.

THE SNAKE

Don't ever make
the bad mistake
of stepping on
the sleeping snake

because
his jaws

might be awake.

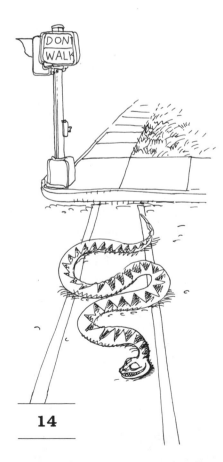

14

THE
CHIPMUNK

Chitter-chatter, chitter-chatter
is the chipmunk's steady patter,
even when he's eating acorns
(which he hopes will make him fatter).

THE MULTILINGUAL MYNAH BIRD

Birds are known to cheep and chirp
and sing and warble, peep and purp,
and some can only squeak and squawk,
but the mynah bird is able to talk.

The mynah bird, the mynah bird,
a major, not a minor bird;
you'll never find a finer bird
than the multilingual mynah bird.

He can talk to you in Japanese,
Italian, French and Portuguese;
and even Russian and Chinese
the mynah bird will learn with ease.

The multilingual mynah bird
can say most any word he's heard,
and sometimes he invents a few
(a very difficult thing to do).

So if you want to buy a bird,
why don't you try the mynah bird?
You'll never find a finer bird
than the multilingual mynah bird.

THE
BENGAL
TIGER

The Bengal tiger likes to eat
enormous quantities of meat.

Now people have been heard to say
that tigers hypnotize their prey.

So please do not take foolish chances;
avoid the Bengal tiger's glances.

THE
EGG

If you listen very carefully, you'll hear the
chicken hatching.
 At first there scarcely was a sound, but
now a steady scratching;
and now the egg begins to crack, the scratching
    starts to quicken,
as anxiously we all await the exit of the chicken.

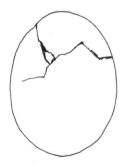

And now a head emerges from the darkness of
    the egg,
and now a bit of fluff appears, and now a tiny leg,
and now the chicken's out at last, he's shaking
    himself loose.
But, wait a minute, that's no chicken . . .
    goodness, it's a goose.

THE
YAK

Yickity-yackity, yickity-yak,
    the yak has a scriffily, scraffily back;
    some yaks are brown yaks and some yaks
  are black,
yickity-yackity, yickity-yak.

Sniggildy-snaggildy, sniggildy-snag,
the yak is all covered with shiggildy-shag;
he walks with a ziggildy-zaggildy-zag,
sniggildy-snaggildy, sniggildy-snag.

Yickity-yackity, yickity-yak,
the yak has a scriffily, scraffily back;
some yaks are brown yaks and some yaks are black,
yickity-yackity, yickity-yak.

SHEEP

Sheep are gentle, shy and meek.
They love to play at hide-and-seek.
Their hearts are softer than their fleece
and left alone they live in peace.

THE
CROCODILE

Beware the crafty crocodile
who beckons you with clever smile
to join him in the river Nile
and swim with him a little while.

His smile is not a friendly smile,
it springs from his dishonest guile
and treacherous reptilian style.
Beware the crafty crocodile.

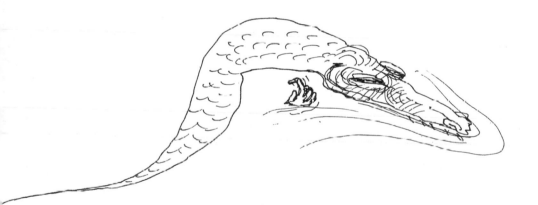

DON'T EVER
SEIZE A WEASEL
BY THE TAIL

You should never squeeze a weasel
for you might displease the weasel,
and don't ever seize a weasel by the tail.

Let his tail blow in the breeze;
if you pull it, he will sneeze,
for the weasel's constitution tends to be
   a little frail.

Yes the weasel wheezes easily;
the weasel freezes easily;
the weasel's tan complexion rather suddenly
 turns pale.

So don't displease or tease a weasel,
squeeze or freeze or wheeze a weasel
and don't ever seize a weasel by the tail.

THE RABBIT

Hip-hop hoppity, hip-hop hoppity,
the rabbit leaps, the rabbit bounds.

28

His ears are long and soft and floppity,
they let him hear the slightest sounds.

THE THREE-TOED SLOTH

The three-toed sloth is in a deep
and curious and wakeless sleep.
The boughs and branches bend and break,
but seldom does the sloth awake.
The noisy jungle far below
is not for three-toed sloths to know.

THE HUMMINGBIRD

The ruby-throated hummingbird is hardly bigger than this WORD.

THE
WALLABY

Oh come and see the wallaby,
  the willy wally wallaby,
   who bounds about so gracefully
with limitless agility.

The wallaby, the wallaby
defies the laws of gravity
and leaps as high as we can see;
the willy wally wallaby.

Oh come and see the wallaby
who runs and jumps unceasingly,
all filled with merriment and glee;
the willy wally wallaby.

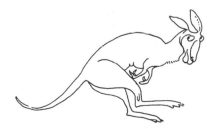

THE TWO—HORNED BLACK RHINOCEROS

The two-horned black rhinoceros
has nothing much to say,
and he tends to be unfriendly and unkind.

He's lumpy and he's grumpy
in a thick-skinned sort of way,
and there's nothing but a grumble on his mind.

THE OSTRICH

The ostrich believes she is hidden from view
with her foolish head stuck in the ground.
For she thinks you can't see her when she
can't see you,
so the ostrich is easily found.

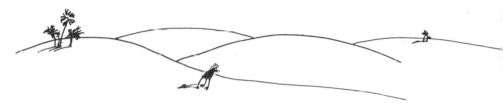

THE GIGGLING GAGGLING GAGGLE OF GEESE

The giggling gaggling gaggle of geese,
they keep all the cows and the chickens awake,
they giggle all night giving nobody peace.
The giggling gaggling gaggle of geese.

The giggling gaggling gaggle of geese,
they chased all the ducks and the swans from the lake.
Oh when will the pranks and the noise ever cease
of the giggling gaggling gaggle of geese!

The giggling gaggling gaggle of geese,
it seems there's no end to the mischief they make,
now they have stolen the sheep's woolen fleece.
The giggling gaggling gaggle of geese.

The giggling gaggling gaggle of geese,
they ate all the cake that the farmer's wife baked.
The mischievous geese are now smug and obese.
The giggling gaggling gaggle of geese.

The giggling gaggling gaggle of geese,
eating that cake was a dreadful mistake.
For when holiday comes they will make a fine feast.
The giggling gaggling gaggle of geese.

THE PACK RAT

The pack rat's day is spent at play
collecting useless stuff.
No matter what the pack rat's got,
he's never got enough.

Nails and tacks and wires and wax,
a knife, a fork, a feather,
large or tiny, dull or shiny,
tin or bone or leather.

Sticks and socks and spoons and rocks
and nuts that squirrels lose,
rings and strings, peculiar things
a rat could never use.

The pack rat saves and stores in caves
strange treasures smooth and knobby.
It's not from greed nor out of need,
he does it as his hobby.

THE
MOLE

The mole's a solitary soul
who minds his own affairs.
He lives contented in a hole
and rarely goes upstairs.

He's blind, so never sees the earth
but trusts his sense of smell,
and burrowing for all he's worth
the mole does very well.

Although it's dank and dark and small
within the mole's domain
and he must tunnel at a crawl,
the mole does not complain.

While other creatures in his place
might feel the urge to roam,
down in his subterranean base
the mole is right at home.

THE PORCUPINE

The porcupine is puzzled
that his friends should act so queer,
for though they come to visit him
they never come too near.

They often stop to say hello
and pass the time of day,
but still the closest of them all
stays many feet away.

He sits and ponders endlessly,
but never finds a clue
to why his close companions
act the distant way they do.

The porcupine has never had
the notion in his brain
that what he finds enjoyable
to others is a pain.

THE BLACK BEAR

In the summer, fall and spring
the black bear sports and has his fling,

but winter sends him straight indoors
and there he snores...and snores...and snores.

THE COW

The cow mainly moos as she chooses
    to moo
    and she chooses to moo as she chooses.

She furthermore chews as she chooses to chew
and she chooses to chew as she muses.

If she chooses to moo she may moo to amuse
or may moo just to moo as she chooses.

If she chooses to chew she may moo as she chews
or may chew just to chew as she muses.

ELECTRIC EELS

Electric eels are rather rude,
they have a shocking attitude
and generate galvanic jolts
of ergs and amperes, watts and volts.

They don't distinguish friend from foe,
to shock and shock is all they know.
So only foolish people feel
a highly tense electric eel.

THE GALLIVANTING GECKO

The gallivanting gecko's ways
are clever and appealing,
he walks up walls and never falls
and trots across the ceiling.

And when he wishes to amaze
the gecko has a knack,
he sheds his tail and without fail
another tail grows back.

THE LION

The lion has a golden mane
and under it a clever brain.
He lies around and idly roars
and lets the lioness do the chores.

THE
BEAVER

The beaver is fat,
    and his tail is so flat
        that it closely resembles an oar.
He's known for his teeth,
those on top and beneath,
and he lives just a trifle offshore.

He nibbles on trees
as a mouse nibbles cheese
with incisors as sharp as a knife.
And with dexterous tricks
builds a house out of sticks
for his children, himself, and his wife.

TOUCANS
TWO

Whatever one toucan can do
is sooner done by toucans two,
and three toucans (it's very true)
can do much more than two can do.

And toucans numbering two plus two can
manage more than all the zoo can.
In short, there is no toucan who can
do what four or three or two can.

THE SNAIL

The snail doesn't know where he's going
and he doesn't especially care,
one place is as good as another
and here is no better than there.

The snail's unconcerned with direction
but happily goes on his way
in search of specifically nothing
at two or three inches a day.

THE HIPPOPOTAMUS

The huge hippopotamus hasn't a hair
on the back of his wrinkly hide;
he carries the bulk of his prominent hulk
rather loosely assembled inside.

The huge hippopotamus lives without care
at a slow philosophical pace,
as he wades in the mud with a thump and a thud
and a permanent grin on his face.

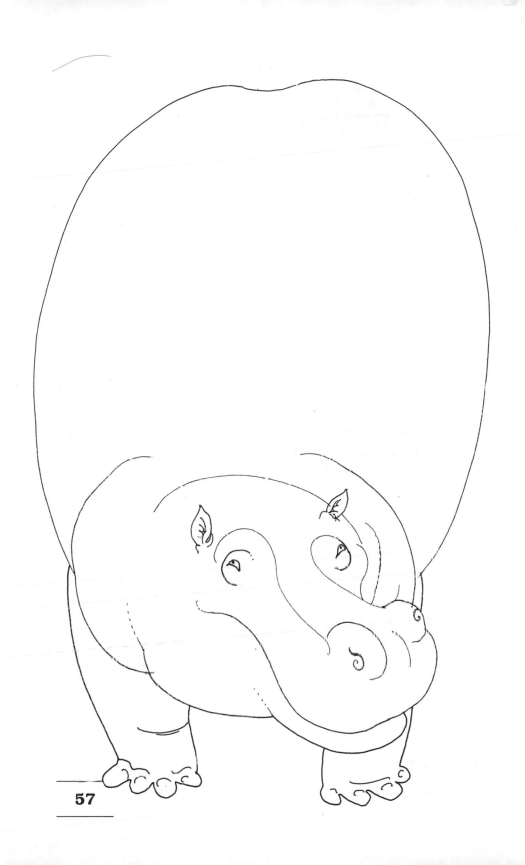

57

THE AARDVARK

The aardvark knows a lot of things,
but seldom has been heard
to say a single syllable
much less an aardvark word.

The aardvark surely would enjoy
the chance to make a sound,
but no one pays attention
when the aardvark comes around.

To so ignore the aardvark
makes the aardvark disinclined
to join in conversation
and reveal what's on his mind.

THE
ZEBRA

The zebra is undoubtedly
a source of some confusion,
his alternating stripes present
an optical illusion.

Observing them is difficult,
one quickly loses track
of whether they are black on white
or rather, white on black.

BEES

Every bee
　　that
　　ever was
was
partly
sting
and partly
... buzz.

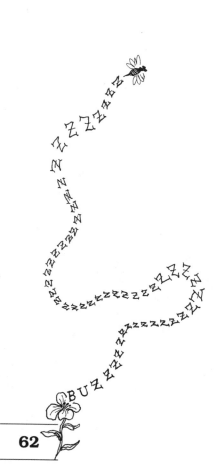

THE HYENA

The laughing hyena's behavior is strange,
for though he does not seek applause
he entertains all within audible range
with his hearty hyena guffaws.

The laughing hyena assembles a crowd
without really having to try;
he opens his mouth and he laughs very loud
but never tells anyone why.

A DROMEDARY
STANDING
STILL

A dromedary standing still
resembles stilts beneath a hill,
and when he lopes along the ground
he seems to be a walking mound.

A herd observed from far away
in lumpy, bumpy disarray
appears to be a very strange
perambulating mountain range.

THE TURLE

The turtle's always been inclined
to live within his shell.
But why he cares to be confined,
the turtle does not tell.

The turtle's always satisfied
to slowly creep and crawl,
and never wanders far outside
his living room or hall.

So if you wish to visit him
in his domestic dome,
just knock politely on his shell,
you'll find the turtle home.

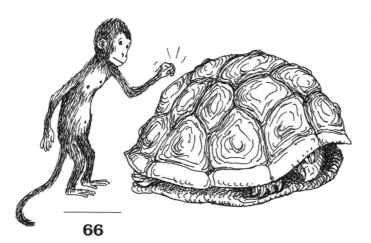

FISH

Fish have fins
and fish have tails;
fish have skins
concealed by scales.
Fish are seldom
found on land;
fish would rather
swim than stand.

THE CHEETAH

The speedy cheetah loves to run,
he's peerless in a race,
for hardly has the race begun
he's finished in first place.

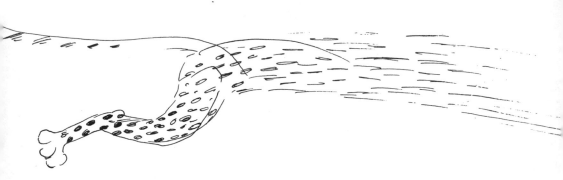

A blur of fur, he dashes past,
he flashes through the air,
the speedy cheetah runs so fast,
before he's here, he's there.

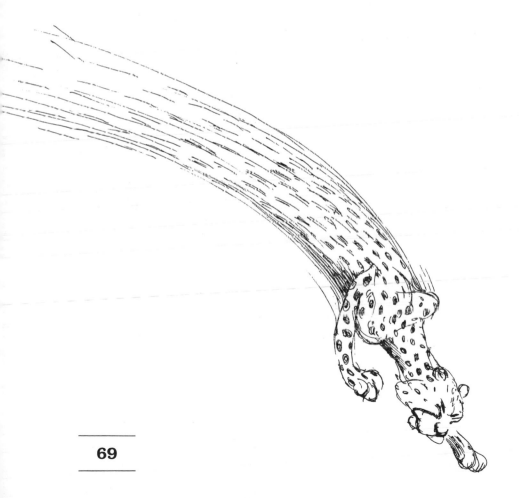

THE ARMADILLO

The ancient armadillo
is as simple as the rain,
he's an armor-plated pillow
with a microscopic brain.

He's disinterested thoroughly
in what the world has wrought,
but spends his time in contemplative,
armadyllic thought.

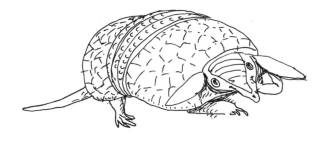

OYSTERS

Oysters
are creatures
without
any features.

OYSTERS

NOT OYSTERS

THE
WALRUS

The widdly, waddly walrus
has flippery, floppery feet.
He dives in the ocean for dinner
and stands on his noggin to eat.

The wrinkly, crinkly walrus
swims with a debonair splash.
His elegant tusks are of ivory
and he wears a fine walrus moustache.

The thundery, blundery walrus
has a rubbery, blubbery hide.
He puffs up his neck when it's bedtime
and floats fast asleep on the tide.

THE CHAMELEON

The changeable chameleon
is forever at his best,
for in any situation
he's appropriately dressed.

Should he stroll through morning flowers
shining golden in the dew,
his attire shortly glitters
with a corresponding hue.

And rambling in the valley
when the meadow grass is green,
he verdantly adjusts himself
and blends into the scene.

In the dim autumnal forest
when the leaves have fallen down,
he corrects his coloration
to a sympathetic brown.

And gazing in the water
he reflects a happy smile,
for the changeable chameleon's
automatically in style.

THE POLAR BEAR

The polar bear by being white
gives up his camouflage at night.
And yet, without a thought or care,
he wanders here, meanders there,
and gaily treads the icy floes
completely unconcerned with foes.
For after dark nobody dares
to set out after polar bears.

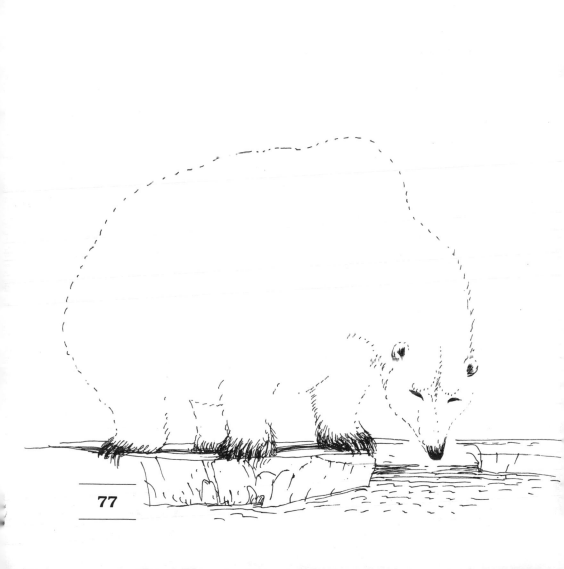

ZOO
DOINGS

In the zoo do view the zebu
doing doings zebus do do.
Do, do view too in the zoo
the kudu doing dos kudus do.

What do zebus that you view do?
Do they do what kudus do do?
Do you view the two? Then you do
view what zebus and kudus do.

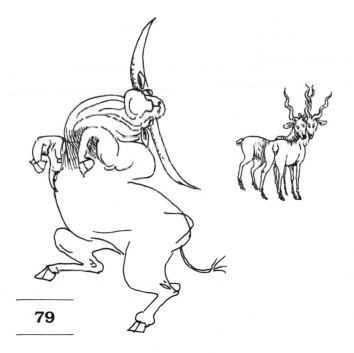

JACK PRELUTSKY was born and raised in New York City but now makes his home in Albuquerque, New Mexico. He has been entertaining young readers for years with his funny and original books of poems, including The Sheriff of Rottenshot, Rolling Harvey down the Hill, It's Halloween, and three ALA Notable Books: The Queen of Eene, The Snopp on the Sidewalk, and Nightmares, a chilling collection of monster poems. He has also translated several books of German and Swedish verse, including The Wild Baby by Barbro Lindgren.

PAUL O. ZELINSKY was born in Evanston, Illinois. He holds a B.A. degree from Yale University and an M.F.A. in Painting from the Tyler School of Art in Pennsylvania. He has adapted and illustrated The Maid and the Mouse and the Odd-shaped House, and is the illustrator of The Sun's Asleep Behind the Hill by Mirra Ginsburg, What Amanda Saw by Naomi Lazard, and How I Hunted the Little Fellows by Boris Zhitkov, an ALA Notable Book.